downtown bookworks

Characters, costumes and settings copyright © 2011 by Maggie Rudy
Text copyright © 2011 by Pam Abrams
Photographs copyright © 2011 by Bruce Wolf

Designed by Georgia Rucker
Typeset in P22 Morris and American Scribe

Printed in China
January 2011

ISBN 978-1-935703-25-9

10 9 8 7 6 5 4 3 2 1

Downtown Bookworks Inc.
285 West Broadway
New York, NY 10013

www.downtownbookworks.com

The House That Mouse Built

BY *Maggie Rudy and Pam Abrams*

PHOTOGRAPHS BY *Bruce Wolf*

downtown bookworks

This is the house
that Mouse built.

This is the cheese, tempting and sweet
Set out in the house that Mouse built.

This is Musetta, fast on her feet
Who stole the cheese, tempting and sweet
Set out in the house that Mouse built.

This is the bumblebee,
black and gold...

That stung Musetta, fast on her feet
Who stole the cheese, tempting and sweet
Set out in the house that Mouse built.

Here is Woolly Bear, small but bold
Who scared the bumblebee, black and gold
That stung Musetta, fast on her feet
Who stole the cheese, tempting and sweet
Set out in the house that Mouse built.

Here is Musetta, with tears in her eyes
Thanking Woolly Bear, small but bold
For scaring the bumblebee, black and gold
That stung Musetta, fast on her feet
Who stole the cheese, tempting and sweet
Set out in the house that Mouse built.

Here is Mouse, who heard her cries
And found Musetta, with tears in her eyes
Thanking Woolly Bear, small but bold
For scaring the bumblebee, black and gold
That stung Musetta, fast on her feet
Who stole the cheese, tempting and sweet
Set out in the house that Mouse built.

Here is the couple — a happy pair

Out and about in the country air...

And here is the judge with long, white hair
Who married the couple — a happy pair
Who fell in love in the country air...

After Mouse heard her cries
And found Musetta, with tears in her eyes
Thanking Woolly Bear, small but bold
For scaring the bumblebee, black and gold
That stung Musetta, fast on her feet
Who stole the cheese, tempting and sweet
Set out in the house that Mouse built.

Now Musetta, Mouse, and Woolly Bear
are very busy as they prepare...

To welcome a baby mouse just born...

Into their house, all cozy and warm.

When Baby is clean from head to toe

He loves to hear tales of long ago

When the kind, old judge with long, white hair,

Married his parents — a happy pair

Who fell in love in the country air

After Mouse heard her cries

And found Musetta, with tears in her eyes

Thanking Woolly Bear, small but bold

For scaring the bumblebee, black and gold

That stung Musetta, fast on her feet

Who stole the cheese, tempting and sweet

Set out in...

...the house that Mouse built.